YOUNG
by K

Illustrated by Gary Andrews

CHARACTERS

Stuart Pedder	a tall, blond boy
Mark Wilkinson	dark-haired, small boy
Lewis McCoy	Stuart's drunken stepfather
Mum, Mrs Pedder	Stuart's mother. In her early forties
Gran, Mrs Wilkinson	Mark's grandmother. In her early eighties
Reg	lorry driver
Sandra	café waitress
Roger **Kyle** **Danny**	} thugs
Vikram **Jemma** **Rachel** **Oswald**	} dossers in a house in Leeds
Nurse	
Reverend Dorkin	
Mr Weaver	friendly old gentleman
Mrs Weaver	kind-hearted old lady
Policeman 1	
Policeman 2	
Hugh Wilkinson	Gran's younger son who lives in Canada

To my Mum, Jessie West, for developing my imagination and confidence

YOUNG RUNAWAYS

ACT ONE
SCENE ONE

Stuart is at home, reading. His mum is drying the supper dishes. There is a heavy tread and both Stuart and his mum look up as a key is turned in the lock. Stuart, no longer reading, appears to be trying to burrow his way into the book. His mum is frightened. A large, grey-haired man enters.

LEWIS: *(half drunk and aggressive)* I just knew you'd love to see me. What a family I have! *(glares at Stuart)* Reading? You'll turn out like your old man. *(shouts)* Put that book away!

MUM: *(gently)* Lewis, don't be harsh on the boy. Reading improves the imagination.

LEWIS: *(scoffing)* Improves the imagination? Aye, and you'll give him funny ideas. You'll place strange thoughts in his mind. *(to Stuart)* Reading isn't for the likes of you and me. You won't earn a penny by reading. Didn't I take down your dad's shelves and throw away all his books? He kept your mum in poverty with his schemes and ideas.

MUM: *(surprised)* Lewis!

LEWIS: *(to mum)* The boy's old enough to know. *(to Stuart)* When your old man died, he left your mum in debt. He hadn't saved a penny. No, not a single penny. Now, you'll be better off working with me on the building sites – get yourself a trade. Reading stories won't do you any good.

STUART: Books take you beyond the ordinary –

LEWIS: Yes, and when you're brought back to the ordinary, like earning your keep, what then? Your old man couldn't cope with that!

STUART: *(stands up clutching his book)* I'm going to my room!

LEWIS: *(blocking the doorway and cruelly mimicking Stuart)* I'm going to my room! What kind of a ponce are you, eh?

(Lewis tries to grab Stuart's book)

Science fiction? You could at least read car manuals, something practical. You'll end up on the dole, you will.

MUM: *(soothing)* Lewis, leave the boy alone.

LEWIS: *(growing irritable, angry)* You'll be a burden to me in my old age. *(strikes out, hitting Stuart across the face)* You'll end up just like your useless old man *(hits Stuart again)* - a great waste of space – full of dreams and ideas that are as worthless as – as ashes in the fire.

(Stuart cries out and falls to the ground.)

MUM:	*(to Lewis)* Look what you've done, you great oaf!
LEWIS:	*(Suddenly quiet, anxious)* Sorry, Stuart, son. The drink's talking. Maybe I'm jealous, maybe you've got something I haven't. *(bends down to Stuart)* Talk to me, son. I only want what's best for you. I only want to set you up in a secure job.
STUART:	*(picks himself up and dabs at his bleeding nose)* Don't even call me son! I'm not your son.
LEWIS:	Sorry, sorry. *(groans miserably)* I didn't mean anything. *(Stuart pushes past Lewis. He runs from the house.)* I didn't mean to hit the boy!

SCENE TWO

Mark is at home with his grandmother, who is frail. She walks with a stick.

GRAN:	You're a good boy, Mark. Do you know, it is five years since my stroke. I couldn't have managed without you. You've helped me to rebuild my life.
MARK:	I know, Gran. You've made a remarkable recovery.

GRAN: *(thinking)* Don't know why I had the stroke. There was no family history – your great-grandparents both lived into their nineties. *(laughs)* Your great-grandad chopped down a big chestnut tree on his ninetieth birthday.

MARK: *(bored)* I've got some homework to do, Gran.

GRAN: On the day I collapsed, my blood pressure was normal. I don't smoke, or drink much. There was just no reason for it. Still, I've rebuilt my life!

MARK: *(anxious)* Mr Dobson, the science teacher will go mad if –

GRAN: *(interrupting)* I got up as usual, went downstairs and that's the last I remember. You found me unconscious on the floor. If you hadn't, I could have died, Mark.

(The doorbell rings.)

MARK: Someone at the door, Gran. I'd better see who it is.

GRAN: If it's the rent man, he can charge me double next week.

(at the door)

MARK: Stuart! Whatever's happened? Your face –

STUART: Stepdad Lewis McCoy strikes again. This time *(indicates bag)* I'm not going back. He hit me last night. This morning, he was snoring on the sofa like a big, fat pig.

MARK: Where will you stay?

STUART: I don't know and I don't care. I'm not going back.

GRAN: *(walks slowly to the door)* Stuart Pedder – come in, how's your dad, how's Graham?

MARK: *(to Gran)* Stuart's dad died, Gran. Remember?

GRAN: *(upset)* Yes…yes, so he did. *(to Stuart)* After my stroke, I rebuilt my life. But I do forget things. Part of my brain was damaged, do you see?

(Gran turns away)

MARK: Sorry…About my gran, mentioning your dad.

STUART: *(shrugs his shoulders)* She's amazing, your gran.

MARK: *(surprised)* Do you think so? *(pause)* I find her annoying.

STUART: After her stroke, when she was in hospital, she couldn't do anything. Now, well, she makes the best of everything.

MARK: *(sullen)* You don't have to live with her!

STUART: Where would you be without her, Mark?

MARK: *(crestfallen)* Taken into care. *(quietly)* It's just that she's –

STUART: *(interrupting)* Yeah, well I'd swap her with Lewis any day. He's so erratic. Sometimes he's fine – a good laugh – and other times he's just violent.

MARK: Sorry. *(pause)* Well, what are you going to do?

STUART: That's up to you, mate.

MARK: What do you mean?

STUART: You once said that if Lewis got really bad, I could sleep in your garage. Now's the time…just for a day or two. Then Mum'll come to her senses and chuck Lewis out. After all, I'm her son. She'd rather have me than that great bear of a man back home.

MARK: *(thinking)* I'm not sure – how can you stay here?

STUART: *(depressed)* I have nowhere else to go. Your gran won't even know.

MARK: Alright mate, just for a day or two.

SCENE THREE

Stuart is asleep on the garage floor. Mark shakes him. Stuart has been in the garage for three days.

MARK: *(Bursting in)* Didn't you hear the commotion?

STUART: *(Yawning and stretching)* What?

MARK: *(peeved)* The ambulance, everything! Gran's had another stroke. She's in hospital. She kept mumbling, hitting the ambulance driver. Nobody could understand what she said. I suppose she would think she made perfect sense to everyone.

STUART: Poor old dear.

MARK: *(concerned)* Where does that leave us?

STUART: *(stretching and yawning)* That leaves us here, until your gran recovers. Suits me!

MARK: You don't understand. We can't stay here.

STUART: *(sitting up)* Why not?

MARK: If Gran recovers, she will have to go into a

home. She won't be able to look after herself again, let alone me. They'll send somebody round in a day or two – the social services.

STUART: *(shocked)* What'll we do?

MARK: Could you return the favour? Could I stay at your place? Two of us to face Lewis?

STUART: No chance.

(silence)

Haven't you got any other relatives?

MARK: Mum and Dad split up and remarried. Neither of them want me, or I wouldn't have stayed with Gran. Gran has a younger son, but he and Dad never got on. I've never met my uncle. *(resigned)* We'll just have to go into care.

STUART: *(determined)* I'm not doing that! We're old enough to look after ourselves. Loads of people younger than us do that.

MARK: Get real!

STUART: I'm deadly serious. We could look after ourselves for a while. I nicked some dosh from Lewis's coat – fifty quid.

MARK: *(whistles)* A thief in our midst!

STUART: I've never stolen before. I reckon Lewis deserved it – he owed me something.

MARK: Gran's got some money stashed away. I don't suppose she'll need it now.

STUART: We'll walk over to the big roundabout near the D.I.Y. place. We'll hitch somewhere north. London's streets were never paved with gold. We'll find ourselves a job and look after each other.

MARK: *(unconvinced)* Sure. We'll become millionaires overnight.

(Much later, under cover of darkness, the two boys hitch out of town. A large container lorry stops for them. They are both feeling very tired.)

REG: 'Op in, boys. Where are you off to?

STUART: The Lake District.

REG: The name's Reg.

(Reg is a thin, dirty-looking man in his early forties. His arms are covered in tattoos.)

Left 'ome 'ave yer, mates? Doin' a runner?

MARK: We're off to see my aunt, who lives up north…a place called Penrith.

REG: What sort of parents 'ave you two got, letting you hitch this time o' night?

STUART: *(lying quickly)* They're away. On business.

REG: *(laughs)* Yeah, well, look after yourselves, mates. I gotta kid myself – around your age. I 'aven't seen my boy for ten years. He's called Dudley, 'cause that's where I met me missus.

STUART: *(sleepily)* Ten years! That's a long time.

REG: Yeah, well! *(laughs)* The job of a lorry driver's a lonesome one. You spend long hours away from 'ome. My missus soon got tired of me being away. She found herself another man down in Weymouth. The hard thing was, she took Dudley with her. *(sighs)* I wonder what he's like now?

(Stuart and Mark are asleep)

Bored the kids to death, I 'ave!

(A few hours later, Reg pulls into a service station.)

(shakes the boys awake) Come on sons, let's 'ave a break.

MARK: Are we in Birmingham?

REG: Not yet, son. We're at a service station. I need a cuppa and something to eat, my belly's rumblin'. Besides, I don't want to stop too near Brummie – there's somebody I want to avoid.

(Reg spits on the ground.)

Big Seamus – the big man 'as a grudge agin me. I don't want a fight, can't afford trouble, don't want to lose me job. *(Reg grins)* Come on, let's get the grub!

(Reg makes off towards the small transport café. He whistles tunelessly as he goes. The boys follow him. The café is full of grim-faced men hunched over cups of tea.)

STUART: *(glares at the interior of the café)* This place looks sleazy.

MARK: None of them look too friendly.

REG: *(walks up to the waitress)* Three teas and three of your bacon sandwiches, Sandra.

SANDRA: Company today, Reg?

REG: *(smiles at the boys)* Yeah, makes a change. The lads are payin'….I don't give free rides.

STUART: *(Takes a five pound note from his pocket)* Here!

REG: *(laughs)* Keep your money, mate. I was only pullin' your leg. Come on, we'll take the spare table.

STUART: Thanks!

MARK: *(picking up his bacon sandwich)* Yeah, thanks. *(To Stuart)* That Sandra, her breath stank.

REG: *(talking and spitting out bacon fat)* Don't you two end up like me. Pass some exams, get some qualifications. This life on the road gets me down. I'm just a modern cowboy – know what I mean?

(the boys nod)

See, I ain't got no 'ome. I got nothin'. All I do is deliver goods. Find yourself a nice wife and kids, and keep 'em.

(Stuart nods. Mark eats his bacon sandwich.)

Yeah, Sandra's breath may stink, but I get so lonely, I think maybe she'll do.

(Just then, the café door swings open. The doorway is filled by a huge man with a great wobbly beer gut. He grunts as he surveys the room.)

Here comes my trouble.

STUART: He looks like he's appeared from somebody's nightmare.

(Seamus McMahon strides over to Reg. His face is an unhealthy red, his flabby chin is covered in black stubble.)

SEAMUS: I want a word with you, Reg Findlay. I followed your cab here. Now it's repayment time.

SANDRA: *(urgent)* Boys, no fights in here. Boys!

REG: *(stands up and looks Big Seamus in the eyes)* Let's settle this outside, Seamus McMahon. *(to the boys)* Go to my cab – here are the keys *(he digs the keys from his jacket pocket)* – and sit inside. Wait for me.

STUART: *(to Mark)* How can thin, puny little Reg compete with such an enemy?

MARK: Stuart – this is none of our business. We just do as the man says, and wait for him.

STUART: But –

MARK: No heroics, Stu, we've got enough trouble of our own.

(The boys walk towards the cab. They hear a large, crashing sound.)

STUART: What was that? Hadn't we better go and see?

MARK: Stu – we stay put and we don't get involved.

(Minutes later, Reg returns. He jumps into his cab and starts the engine.)

REG: Come on boys, what are you waiting for? Let's get the show on the road. A lesson for you two boys – never pick a fight if you've 'ad too much booze.

STUART: What happened?

REG: *(feeling proud)* Oh, I danced round 'im like Mohammed Ali used to do, while he growled like Tyson. Then I 'it 'im with me nut. *(Reg taps his head)* 'E won't bother me again. The fuzz'll 'ave 'im for drink-drivin'. *(Reg laughs)* reckon I broke 'is nose. Told you I didn't want trouble, but if it comes my way, I'll deal with it. Right, mates?

STUART: *(enthusiastic)* Yeah.

MARK: *(unconvinced)* Sure.

STUART: What did Big Seamus McMahon want you for?

REG: Ask no questions, I'll tell you no lies.

(A while and two lifts later, the boys are hitching near Preston when a van pulls up. A leather-jacketed, black-booted youth grins out of the window.)

ROGER: Room for two more in the back. Just pull the handle down and jump in. Where are you two off to?

STUART & MARK: The Lake District.

ROGER: The very place we're making for.

(Inside the van, there are two other youths, in their late teens.)

KYLE: These greenhorns are ripe for the picking, eh Roger?

ROGER: *(warning)* Not yet, Kyle.

STUART: *(to Mark)* What does he mean?

MARK: I don't know, but I don't like what I hear.

KYLE: *(smoking – and blowing smoke in the boys' faces)* Ah, you'll just have to excuse me. I've a wicked sense of humour, haven't I Danny?

DANNY: *(looks across while driving the van)* Kyle has a wicked sense of humour.

MARK: Could you stop the van? We'd rather walk.

ROGER: *(laughing)* Now that is seriously funny. Walk? All the way to the Lakes? Get real.

STUART: *(afraid)* Please…We'd like to try.

KYLE: *(indicating Danny)* He can't stop on the motorway, can you Danny? It's against regulations, ain't it Roger?

ROGER: Too right. We'd be nicked.

(The three youths laugh.)

MARK: Why are you turning off the M6?

ROGER: *(to Kyle)* This one's perceptive.

DANNY: *(laughing)* Sharp boy, he'd make a good copper.

ROGER: *(leering at Mark and Stuart)* Now's the time to let you into our little secret.

DANNY: *(sniggering)* We're not going to the Lakes.

KYLE: *(finding everything amusing)* We're going to Leeds.

(The three black-clad youths laugh.)

ROGER: We're going to do a job.

KYLE: You two are our little side-line.

MARK: *(Worried)* What do you mean, side-line?

KYLE: We drop you off at Leeds –

ROGER: Unharmed –

DANNY: But you give us your dosh.

STUART: You can't do this, it…it's illegal.

KYLE: Illegal! Got that, Roger!

DANNY: *(driving carelessly)* Listen sonny – everything we do is illegal.

MARK: *(quickly)* We don't have any money.

STUART: *(thinking fast)* We're broke...we're dossers.

KYLE: *(sniggering)* Then you won't mind me going through your bags, will you?

MARK: *(quickly)* We do have some money, Stuart's custodian.

KYLE: How much?

MARK: *(quickly)* Fifty quid.

ROGER: That'll do us.

(The van grinds to a halt.)

KYLE: Give!

(Stuart hands over the wallet, full of notes, all the money he took from Lewis's coat.)

DANNY: *(leaning over from the driver's seat)* Now – get out of our van, sharpish.

(He kicks Stuart. The van starts up as Stuart and Mark are pushed out into the roadway.)

ROGER: Bye bye. Sweet dreams!

MARK: Did you get the registration number?

STUART: No. Didn't you?

MARK: I don't think they had one.

STUART: We're lucky to be alive.

MARK: They're lucky to have over fifty quid.

STUART: My fifty quid.

MARK: *(practical)* We'll share the rest. I took sixty quid from Gran's room. At least they didn't get the lot. We're about ten miles from Leeds.

STUART: How do you know?

MARK: We passed a signpost about four miles past.

STUART: We'll walk.

MARK: It's raining.

STUART: I'm not hitching again.

SCENE FOUR

At Stuart's home. Mum is crying. She is reading a letter Stuart has written for her, before he left home.

MUM: *(to Lewis)* A week and no sign of the boy. You were too hard on him, Lewis, too harsh.

LEWIS: I only meant for the best. I didn't mean the boy any harm.

MUM: You never understood Stuart - you wanted to make him into a different person.

LEWIS: *(pouring himself a glass of whisky)* He was a dreamer, always a dreamer.

MUM: And you can't make a square peg fit into a round hole.

LEWIS: *(stubborn)* I didn't want the boy turning out like his old man.

MUM: So – with your drink and your violence and your coldness, you tried to destroy Stuart Pedder, because…because he was different. His dad was a gentle, kind man. He gave Stuart a home full of books.

LEWIS: *(sniggers)* Graham Pedder was like a minstrel who entertains at a banquet and departs leaving the dishes unwashed. I've had to provide. Without me, you'd be poor. He left you nothing.

MUM: *(determined)* Well, Lewis, if you don't find Stuart, you and your money can go.

SCENE FIVE

Stuart and Mark have found an old derelict house outside Leeds. They creep in, through a broken door, to shelter from the heavy rain.

STUART: We'll doss down here for a while.

MARK: *(looking around)* Yeah – except somebody else already has. There are sleeping bags on the floor – and dirty clothes.

(Four scruffy-looking youths enter.)

VIKRAM: *(indicating Mark and Stuart)* Look what the rain's brought in!

JEMMA: We was 'aving the place to ourselves.

RACHEL: *(nudging Jemma)* Me Mam told me never to trust strangers.

OSWALD: *(quietly spoken. He has a cultured accent.)* Just a minute – they could be useful, you three are always too hasty.

JEMMA: *(looking closely at Stuart)* He's cute!

VIKRAM: *(jealous)* That does it, they leave.

OSWALD: No, no, Vikram old boy, they stay. We need them.

JEMMA: It were a right do today, we made nothing. Perhaps *(looking at Stuart)* the cute one can help.

STUART: *(picks up his rucksack)* We're leaving, right Mark?

RACHEL: Get a load of that – southerners. Must be right rich kids, me Mam said…

OSWALD: Forget the north-south divide, old girl. There are rich and poor everywhere. We share and share alike here.

VIKRAM: Who said?

OSWALD: I say, old chum – and I'm boss here.

JEMMA: *(to Stuart and Mark)* Oswald thinks he's it, just 'cause he went to a posh school, but he's no job… same as us.

STUART: *(shocked)* Do you…do you live here?

VIKRAM: This is our squat.

RACHEL: Until we're kicked out.

JEMMA: Rachel's right… welcome to our temporary 'ome.

OSWALD: Better than sleeping rough, on the streets, my young friends.

RACHEL: Catch your death of cold on the pavements.

JEMMA: The wind goes right through yer.

OSWALD: Right young chaps – tomorrow you are on the streets with Rachel.

SCENE SIX

Stuart, Mark and Rachel are on the streets, begging. Rachel has a flute. She is a good player. She plays Bob Dylan tunes. Passers-by throw coins in a hat that Mark holds.

RACHEL: *(to Mark)* Like it 'ere love?

MARK: *(jumping up and down to keep warm)* It's freezing.

RACHEL: Tough life – eh?

STUART: Yeh.

RACHEL: Why not go 'ome, love?

STUART: Nobody wants me. My stepdad beats me up.

RACHEL: *(looks at him hard)* You're – you're Stuart Pedder, aren't you? *(to passer-by who drops a twenty-pence piece in the hat)* Thanks, love, have a nice day.

STUART: *(shocked)* How do you know who I am?

RACHEL: *(touches her nose)* I know everything, love…. 'Ere comes a rich bloke, his shoes are well polished. Me mam used to say – oh, never mind.

MARK: *(suspicious)* How did you know about Stu?

RACHEL: *(takes paper from under her woollen jumper)* Here, take a look.

STUART: *(reading)* 'Missing. Can you help?' *(to Mark)* Look, they've got my grotty old school photograph in here.

MARK: Your mum wants you back. Maybe you should 'phone.

RACHEL: Anything's better than this, love. *(to another passer-by)* Thanks love, have a nice day. Hey, we've made £5, lovvies! I'll tell you something – it's good when a Christian passes by.

STUART: Why's that?

RACHEL: Well, you see, they say God bless…and you need blessin', don't yer? It's a real tough world.

MARK: *(thoughtful)* Yeah.

RACHEL: And if you're lucky, like, they'll stop and chat and buy yer a hot drink or sommat.

STUART: *(shivering)* Right.

RACHEL: To think I'm a Scouse. Born in Bootle down by the docks. We're supposed to have nouse, us Liverpudlians. And here I am, beggin', and me mam used to take me to the Isle of Man *(reflecting)* for me 'olidays. Then I got abused by 'er lover, so I left.

STUART: *(shivering)* Yeah.

RACHEL: Well, Oswald – Ossie – he's got the gift of the gab. He'll either end up a millionaire, or in clink. The bussies are on to him.

STUART: Bussies?

RACHEL: Police. *(looks ahead)* Hey-up, 'ere comes one now.

POLICEMAN: *(kind)* Hello love, seen you before, 'aven't I?

RACHEL: *(defiant)* Yeah.

POLICEMAN: Told you before, you can't stop 'ere.

RACHEL: Against the law, is it?

POLICEMAN: *(calm)* Yeah, now shift.

RACHEL: No trouble, me. Come on kids, we'll move.

(Policeman talks into the walkie-talkie as they depart.)

MARK: What now?

RACHEL: We'll see what the others are doing.

SCENE SEVEN

Back at the squat

OSWALD: Rachel, glad to see you, old girl.

RACHEL: Yeah, I bet.

OSWALD: It's Vikram. He's had a bad fix.

JEMMA: *(distressed)* He's sweating, swearing and crying.

VIKRAM: *(shouts)* Worms all over me. They're oozing out of the walls.

RACHEL: You shouldn't 'ave got that cheap stuff, Oswald.

JEMMA: He's shivering – he's passing out.

RACHEL: What'll we do, Ossie love?

OSWALD: *(nasty)* How should I know, dearie? I'm not a doctor.

JEMMA: Eh, shouldn't we call one – or an ambulance, or sommat?

OSWALD: You crazy? And blow all my plans away?

RACHEL: Vikram's our mate.

OSWALD: *(very nasty)* We have no friends, only alliances.

JEMMA: *(tearful)* He's my friend.

RACHEL: We told 'im to ease up on the drugs.

OSWALD: *(matter of fact)* Yes, but they are the only comfort you have to make your sad lives bearable.

STUART: *(to Mark)* Drugs? We've got to get out of here.

MARK: And go where, Stu?

OSWALD: *(to Mark)* Sensible boy. Somebody after my own heart, at last. You'll like my little scam.

JEMMA: Don't tell the boy, Ossie.

OSWALD: Oh why not? I like to blow my own

	trumpet. Why should I hide my light under a bushel? *(to Mark)* I pass off as an insurance agent. My accent is such, old ladies trust me. They pay a deposit, I simply vanish. I've made thousands of pounds, dear boy. Now wouldn't you like to help me?
MARK:	*(considering)* Well!
STUART:	*(firmly)* NO!
RACHEL:	Ossie love, Vikram's bad.
OSWALD:	Time to split!
RACHEL:	What's happened to Vikram, could have happened to you.
OSWALD:	Oh no, sorry to disappoint you, old girl. But I keep the pure stuff for myself. He who contributes the most gets the best.
	(A police siren is heard.)
RACHEL:	Bussies – a raid.
OSWALD:	Time to split.
RACHEL:	That policeman I saw – he must have followed me here.
OSWALD:	Tut, tut. Careless Rachel. *(he opens a window)* We'll leave Vikram and escape down the drainpipe.

JEMMA: *(scared)* It's a right bad do is this. Nowt's goin' right.

RACHEL: *(to Mark and Stuart)* Go on boys, up the stairs and on to the roof. You can get clear.

(the boys do as they are told)

POLICEMAN: *(enters)* Now what have we here?

RACHEL: *(She points to Vikram)* Call us an ambulance, love.

(Oswald climbs down the drainpipe. A second policeman is waiting for him in the shadows.)

POLICEMAN 2: Not so fast, Oswald Prendergast.

(Stuart and Mark escape along the roof and in through a broken window of another derelict house.)

STUART: I thought those squatters were decent people.

MARK: Dream on!

STUART: I mean – Rachel.

MARK: *(concerned)* If we don't do something *(indicates next door)* that is our future! We'll either end up selling 'The Big Issue' or we'll beg our lives away on street corners. We need to do something practical – to lift ourselves out of this mess.

ACT TWO
SCENE ONE

The hospital. Gran is sitting up in bed. Her younger son, Hugh Wilkinson, is sitting in a chair by her bedside. He has a slight Canadian accent.

GRAN: *(cheerful)* Hugh, have you come back to help me rebuild my life?

HUGH: Yes, Mum. I've come to take you home, to Canada. You can live with me from now on. You can live in our annexe.

GRAN: *(disgusted)* A granny flat, Hugh? Is that what it all boils down to?

HUGH: *(patient)* You have had two strokes, Mum. You might have been in real trouble if you hadn't had time to phone for an ambulance.

GRAN: *(confused)* I didn't call the ambulance, Hugh. *(becomes very agitated)* Somebody else did. I can't remember who. *(tearful)* Somebody else called the ambulance.

NURSE: Now don't go and upset yourself, Mrs Wilkinson.

34

GRAN:	*(confused)* Somebody else lived with me, you don't understand. You lived in Australia, we lost touch.
HUGH:	Canada. I live in Canada, Mum.
GRAN:	*(remembering)* Mark! Where's Mark? *(to Hugh)* Your nephew. He lives with me. Where is he? *(worried)* He's gone!
HUGH:	*(concerned)* Tell me as much as you can remember, Mum. I'll go and investigate.

SCENE TWO

Lewis and Stuart's mother are standing outside Mark's grandmother's house.

MUM:	There are people inside Mrs Wilkinson's house. Up to no good, I expect. I'll call the police.
LEWIS:	*(determined)* Yes, but I'd better have a look around now.
MUM:	*(squeezes Lewis's hand)* Oh Lewis, take care! *(Lewis goes into the house just as Mr Wilkinson walks along the road, looking for Gran's house.)*
MUM:	Oh, excuse me. Could you help us? There seems to be a spot of trouble.

HUGH: Trouble?

MUM: There are intruders in old Mrs Wilkinson's house. My…my… *(she cannot bring herself to say 'boyfriend')* my friend is investigating.

HUGH: I'll go and take a look. Here, take my mobile and call the police.

(Inside Gran's house, Lewis is talking to Kyle, Roger and Danny.)

LEWIS: *(holding Stuart's wallet)* Explain to me again, how did you get hold of Stuart Pedder's wallet?

KYLE: *(unafraid)* We threatened him and his mate. We took the wallet and dumped them near Leeds. He had this address so we thought we'd burgle the place. We even had the keys – but they didn't fit.

LEWIS: *(shouting)* That's because they're the keys to my house.

DANNY: *(cheeky)* Watch yourself, fat man. Think of your blood pressure. You'll have a heart attack.

ROGER: Yeah, take care, bag of guts.

(Mr Wilkinson walks in unnoticed.)

HUGH: Right! *(to the boys and thinking quickly)* You are all under arrest. This place is surrounded.

ROGER: *(panicking)* We can't make a run for it, we're done for.

KYLE: *(to Danny)* I told you we should have thrown the wallet away, didn't I?

DANNY: *(depressed)* Just shut up, will you?

LEWIS: *(to Hugh)* Stuart and Mark were last seen in Leeds. Fancy a long drive?

HUGH: As soon as we have dealt with these three.

SCENE THREE

Stuart and Mark are walking through Leeds town centre.

STUART: I'm hungry, and I want to know what's happened to Rachel.

MARK: *(moody)* Why don't you just shut up about Rachel? There are hundreds of Rachels up and down the country – hundreds all living rough.

STUART: *(sees a church)* Let's try to find help here, in the church. People seek sanctuary in a church.

MARK: *(coughs)* I'll try anything. The rain's getting to me. *(coughs)* My chest is bad and I've run out of capsules for my inhaler.

STUART: Have you got a problem I don't know about?

MARK: Just mild asthma… but the damp's getting to me.

(Inside the church, the boys see a vicar.)

REV DORKIN: *(half afraid)* Boys, what are you doing here? I've had enough of you vandals. Last month it was the stained glass windows. What now?

STUART: We don't want to harm your windows, or anything else here, Rev.

REV DORKIN: Reverend Dorkin, that's my name.

STUART: My mate is sick and –

REV DORKIN: You're not from this area are you? You speak like a southerner.

STUART: We got lost in Leeds and –

MARK: *(coughing)* Tell him the truth, Stu!

STUART: *(quickly)* We've run away from home and we have no money, no food, no….

REV DORKIN: There are many like you, out in the streets.

STUART: My mate's ill and –

REV DORKIN: *(quickly)* Look, I have to arrange a wedding. But – er – I can give you an address.

(Later, having walked through the cold, damp streets, the friends arrive at a place for disadvantaged people. Inside is a kindly, plump lady who wears glasses.)

Mrs WEAVER: I have some hot soup. It's right cold outside. Right parky day out there.

(Inside, the place is empty, except for a man in his early seventies. He is filling in forms.)

Here Frank, leave those forms alone and do something practical.

Mr WEAVER: *(leaves the forms)* Right! *(he looks inside various cupboards)* Mary, where are the soup cups?

Mrs WEAVER: Oh Frank, they're where you put them last. *(to the boys)* Honestly, that man's memory!

(Mark collapses)

Oh dear *(she attends Mark)* Frank, leave the cups, can't you see there is an emergency? Call an ambulance. Before you ask, the telephone is up the stairs on the right. *(to Stuart)* We've only just started helping out here. It's all voluntary, you know. Frank will have to hold the fort – he's so absent-minded he isn't much use. Well, there's nowt going on here, so I'll come to the hospital with you.

(Later, at the hospital)

MARK: Where's Mrs Weaver?

STUART: Gone.

MARK: *(still chesty)* What are we going to do? We can't live on dreams, can we? Is that what we are condemned to for the rest of our lives?

(Walking through the ward is Rachel. She is holding a bunch of flowers.)

RACHEL: *(to Mark)* Thought you'd like these, luv. They're special, fell off the back of a lorry. Mrs Weaver told me you were here.
The men in blue released me and guess what, I landed a job as a film extra in the Isle of Man! Who's a lucky girl? Isn't that brilliant! Me, an actress!

STUART: *(quietly)* You're pretty enough.

RACHEL: *(to Mark)* Cor! Get him! Hey, I'll be on the telly next, I will. Wish me mam could see me. They're going to put Ossie away for some time. And, oh yeah, Vikram's getting treatment. *(She places the flowers carefully on Mark's bed.)* Got to go. *(waves enthusiastically)* Ta ra! Tell you what though, if this 'extra' thing works out, I'll come back and take you to the Isle of Man.

STUART: *(enthusiastic)* Yeah, yeah, do that!

RACHEL: *(skipping out of the ward)* Ta ra, boys!

(Almost bumping into Rachel are Lewis McCoy and Hugh Wilkinson)

STUART: Oh no, Lewis!

LEWIS: *(kindly)* Stuart, listen please. I owe you an apology, son. And I'm trying to kick the drinking habit. Really I am. I want you to come home.

HUGH: *(to Mark)* Mark, I'm your uncle, your father's brother. We need to talk.

MARK: Gran – is she –

HUGH: Your gran will be fine after physiotherapy – but she's old, Mark. She needs looking after. I'm taking the both of you to Canada.

SCENE FOUR

Gran's house, a month later. Stuart, Mark and Hugh are talking.

HUGH: *(to Mark)* Your gran won't move to Canada, Mark. She claims she's too old and too settled in her ways. If Mohammed won't go to the mountain, the mountain must come to Mohammed. So I'm getting a company transfer back to England. My wife Sue and I are buying the grand old house on the hill.

MARK: Gate Lodge?

HUGH: Yes. I've made plenty of money, but money is useless unless you do something with it. So I'm going to help look after my mother.

MARK: Do I go into care?

HUGH: *(smiling)* Sue and I always wanted children. Sadly, that was not to be. We'd like you to stay with us, Mark. Perhaps, in time, we could talk about adoption.

MARK: *(laughing)* Yes – oh yes.

HUGH: And how are things working out for you, Stuart?

STUART: *(cheerful)* They're settled. Lewis has gone into a rehabilitation clinic and mum and I are working things out. But –

HUGH: Yes?

STUART: Mark and I are two of the lucky ones. There are thousands of young people out there who are homeless, friendless.... Victims of society. *(determined)* When I grow up, I want to do something about it. I want a country where nobody sleeps rough.

MARK: Dream on!

HUGH: We need dreams, Mark, if we are to change things for the better.

YOUNG RUNAWAYS

ACTIVITIES
ACT ONE: SCENES ONE AND TWO

Discussion
Lewis has a great deal of criticism against Stuart and his dad. What is the criticism and what is Stuart's defence?

Can you see that scene one is allegorical? Look at how Lewis and Stuart's views on education differ. Are Lewis and Stuart stereotypes, or are their characters portrayed in a way that we can view them as individuals? What are your views on the values of reading?

Mark is unable to communicate with his gran in the early part of scene two. What does Gran think of as important in her life? What does Mark believe is immediately important for his life?

Why does Stuart find Mark's gran amazing and why do you think Mark is taken by surprise?

Improvisation
Imagine you are Lewis. You are talking to some mates at work. What do you tell them about Stuart and his dead father? You point out that you lost your temper with Stuart and hit him. How might your workmates react?

Writing
Use the library to research the causes and effects of a stroke. Find out about societies that help stroke victims. Write a social worker's report on Gran. Do you think she is able to look after herself or does she need help?
and/or
Use the library to find out about drink-related problems such as violent behaviour. Write a social worker's report on Lewis.

ACT ONE: SCENES THREE AND FOUR

Artwork
Draw a 'wanted' poster for either Seamus or Kyle. Underneath, state what they have done wrong. Use your imaginations.

Freeze-framing
In small groups, freeze-frame the moment when Mark and Stuart are pushed into the roadway and the gang peer out of the van (end of scene three). What will Mark and Stuart feel like? Can their feelings be expressed by the way they look? The gang will be pleased with themselves. Can you convey their feelings through body language and looks?

Improvisation
When Reg is asked about why Seamus McMahon wants him, he is evasive. Improvise a scene in which Seamus and Reg fall out. It could be over some sort of scam, or a tiff over a girl they both like. You decide and improvise the scene.

Hot-seating
Try to remember as many facts as possible. In groups of three or four, hot-seat the following characters.

Lewis - what does he feel towards learning and does he regret acting violently towards Stuart?

Roger - is he proud of being part of a violent gang? What are his hopes and plans for the future?

Mark - is he beginning to regret leaving Gran? Does he wonder how she is doing in hospital? How does he differ from Stuart, and will these differences matter?

Mum - does she have any regrets about marrying Lewis? Why did she marry somebody so different in character and temperament from her first husband? What are her thoughts now that Stuart has left home?

SCENE FOUR

Discussion
Re-read the talk between Lewis and Mum (towards the end of scene four).

What did Lewis mean when he said that Graham Pedder was, 'like a minstrel who entertains at a banquet and departs leaving the dishes unwashed.' Did it surprise you that Lewis would speak using metaphorical language?

Mum told Lewis that 'you can't make a square peg fit into a round hole.' She uses metaphorical language. What did she mean and what effect is the playwright trying to have on the audience by using such language?

Writing
What words would you use to describe the following characters?

Character	Description	Evidence
Lewis	Violent	Scene one. He hit Stuart.
Reg		
Seamus		
Mark		
Stuart		
Gran		

Danny, Roger and Kyle claim that robbing the boys was just a sideline. Write about their 'main job'. It could be a bank robbery or a credit-card scam. Whatever you think the three are about to do, write about it!

SCENE FIVE

Discussion
New characters are introduced in scene five. Look at the

following characters:
Jemma
Rachel
Vikram
Oswald

What do we learn about the new characters? Who appears kind, who appears cruel? What do you imagine the characters to look like? Which characters are we meant to have sympathy for and/or empathy with? If not, can you think of better names for each character?

Hot-seating.
Hot-seat the following characters.

Oswald - How does he feel after his capture by the police? What are his feelings towards the others, himself?

Rachel - Why do you think Rachel stays with Vikram rather than look after herself? How does she feel towards Mark and Stuart? What are her feelings towards Oswald?

Stuart - He is very different from Mark. What does he feel about the situation now? What are his hopes and plans for the future? How does he feel about the squatters, and Rachel?

Writing
Write a police report on Oswald. You may use evidence from the play and your imagination.

Use the library to find out all you can about homeless people. Now write a social worker's report on the homeless situation in Britain. (You may want to look at recently published fiction books on the subject such as 'Stone Cold' by Robert Swindle and 'Homebird' by Terence Blacker.)

ACT TWO: SCENES ONE TO FOUR

Discussion
Do you think the end was realistic, unrealistic, optimistic, pessimistic, exciting, an anti-climax? What was the playwright's main aim in writing the play?

Storyboarding
Choose any three key events from scenes one to four and storyboard them - as if you were making a film of 'Young Runaways'. Sketch each frame and describe what the audience will hear.

Improvisation
In small groups, choose a scene you like best in Act Two and improvise that scene, bringing out the way the characters speak, and the action.

Writing
You are Hugh. Write your thoughts and feelings down in your diary, from when you meet Gran until you decide to look after Stuart.

You are Lewis, you write to Stuart from the rehabilitation centre. Explain your thoughts and feelings about the future.

Discussion
When you are familiar with the whole play, make a list of the main plot and all the sub-plots. Do others agree with you? Which is the most powerful plot in the play? Why?